The Cuckoo's Sacrifice

A Tale from the Yucatán

by Joseph da Silva   illustrated by Tom Leonard

 HOUGHTON MIFFLIN   BOSTON

Have you ever noticed how brightly colored most birds in the Yucatán are? A peninsula in southeastern Mexico, the Yucatán is famous for its unique mangrove forests, where more than three hundred species of birds make their home. There you see gorgeous parrots with crimson heads and bright blue wing feathers. Long-legged flamingoes flock to the shores. Yucatán jays make an impression with their black bodies, yellow beaks, and wings of vibrant blue. Bright green macaws wear yellow feather necklaces. And, if you're lucky, you might glimpse the colorful toucans, with their giant bills, hiding among the forest's emerald leaves.

However, if you manage to spot a cuckoo, you can't help but notice that this bird is not colorful like the others. Instead, its feathers are a dull gray. The bird doesn't sound as glorious as the others, either, having more of a bark than a musical song.

Yet the unassuming cuckoo is a genuine hero to other birds, and its drab color and rough voice are part of the reason.

Many, many years ago, before calendars kept track of time, the cuckoo was as brightly colored as any bird in the forest. Indeed, she was always considered one of the most beautiful birds. Not only did she have feathers of scarlet and gold and blue and green, but she also had a lovely, musical voice.

At that time, however, she was not seen as heroic, and for good reason.

Although the cuckoo was splendid on the outside, her character was not equally attractive. If the truth be told, the cuckoo was actually rather foolish. She was quite vain about her appearance, and sometimes she acted a bit lazy. She would spend most of her time singing songs to herself and preening her feathers. She always waited until the last minute to find food and build a nest. Now, these are not horrible qualities, but they did keep the cuckoo from earning the respect that many other birds of the forest enjoyed.

Other airborne residents would fly about, building solid nests, gathering food, and generally doing good works, while the cuckoo would perch on a treetop and practice her songs. Her voice was certainly beautiful, but many of the other birds resented her for practicing tunes while they did chores.

One day, the rain god, Chak, appeared in the forest to assemble the birds. He wore shells on his head and in his ears, and he carried his ceremonial axe.

"Tomorrow is the day of the annual seed harvest," Chak said, "when we flock to the fields to gather up all the seeds that we will need to plant next year. Once again, I ask for your participation."

The birds held this harvest every autumn, and it was an event of vital importance. Every bird flew far and wide, searching for favorite seeds. Some gathered wheat, some collected maize, and others harvested the seeds of delicate grasses. These seeds were then assembled in an enormous heap and stored for next year's planting. If no bird gathered seeds from a particular plant, then that plant would forever cease to exist. Every bird in the forest knew that his or her future survival depended on this seed harvest.

Chak continued. "We will start at daybreak tomorrow, and I want everyone to be prompt. This season of the year is dry, and fire is a constant possibility. As soon as the seeds are safely harvested, I can distribute rain everywhere to reduce the fire hazard."

The birds listened intently, except for the cuckoo, who was busy preening her tail feathers. Most birds shuddered when they heard the word *fire*, because forest wildlife is terrified of fire. The birds' uneasy rustling and squawking attracted the cuckoo's attention.

"What did he say?" the cuckoo asked no one in particular as she looked around vaguely. "What are we supposed to be doing? Sorry, but I wasn't really paying attention."

The scarlet macaw stood on one foot and pointed two scaly toes at the cuckoo. "You must pay attention," he warned, "because all our lives depend on it."

The cuckoo's scarlet cheeks blazed even brighter than before. "Sorry," she said again.

Now it was the parrot's turn to scold. "Last year, cuckoo, you arrived late, after most of the work was finished! You pull that kind of stunt again, and no one will have any respect for you at all."

Again, the cuckoo said, "Sorry," and this time she tucked her head under her wing.

"Enough squabbling!" called Chak sternly. "We need to protect each other, not pick each other to pieces. Tomorrow is going to be a long day, everyone. Now get to bed early, because you'll need to feel rested in the morning."

That night, all the birds went to their nests and slept soundly—all except the cuckoo. She was embarrassed by the scolding that she had received, yet she secretly knew that she deserved it. In the past, she had not really done as much work as the others, nor had she taken their problems seriously. She promised herself that, from this moment on, she would try to be a responsible citizen of the forest.

The next morning, the birds of the Yucatán awoke to confusion. Thick black smoke filled the heavens. The forest was ablaze! In the underbrush, flames licked the trunks of the trees, and the dry grasses fueled the fire. The heat was so intense and the roar of the fire so deafening that the terrified birds were driven toward the shoreline. There they huddled together near the water's edge to plan what to do next.

At first, they felt relieved that they had escaped with their lives. Then the parrot moaned, saying, "We're doomed! The fire came before the annual seed harvest! Chak was not able to bring the rain in time to save the seeds! Now we won't have any food for next year! We're all going to die of starvation!"

With growing horror, the others realized that the parrot was right. Not only would their homes in the trees be destroyed, but also the fire had stolen their chance to gather the seeds that were necessary for their survival. The birds exchanged frantic looks and began to argue about what they should do next. Then, a small movement in the sky caught their attention.

From the center of one billowing cloud of smoke, a single bird slowly soared. It was an unfamiliar gray and sooty bird whose feathers had been scorched by the fire's fierce heat. It carried a large packet in its bill, and it flew right into the safety of a cave by the water's edge.

When the bedraggled bird emerged from the cave a few minutes later, the others beckoned it to join them. When the bird fluttered down, they were amazed to discover its identity. Even the flamingoes waded closer to take a look at the new arrival. A pair of jays found a leaf with fresh water and brought it over for the exhausted bird to drink. It was the cuckoo, but she looked very different from the day before.

"Cuckoo, what happened? Where have you been?" asked the toucan. All the other birds anxiously waited in silence. They all wanted to hear cuckoo's story.

Cuckoo opened her mouth to speak, but instead of her glorious song, only a croak emerged. Her throat had been singed by the terrible heat, and her voice was now harsh and rough.

"I was so worried about oversleeping," she whispered, "that I couldn't fall asleep. I felt guilty about being lazy in the past, and I wanted to prove to you all that I can do my fair share of the work. Just after midnight, I smelled smoke, and I realized that a fire had broken out somewhere. I flew to the fields to gather up as much wheat and maize and other seeds as I could. I knew how important the harvest was, so I worked all night gathering seeds and carrying them to the cave, where I knew they would be safe. I was so busy flying back and forth, I had no idea how far the fire had spread until I saw all of you rushing toward the shore."

In a rush of wings, all the birds flew to the cave. They were stunned to see that it was filled with every kind of seed in the forest. They turned again to the cuckoo, realizing how badly they had misjudged the little bird. They knew that she was as terrified of fire as they were. Yet she had overcome her fear for the sake of all the birds of the forest.

"You risked your life for us," said the macaw. "You sacrificed your gorgeous feathers so that we could eat next year. Why didn't you alert someone?"

"No time," answered the cuckoo simply. Then, suddenly, she realized what else the macaw had said. She looked at herself carefully. "My feathers! What's happened to my feathers?" she wailed. Until that moment, she had not known that she was no longer a beautiful, brightly colored bird.

The cuckoo looked again at her dull, gray feathers and burst out crying. "Oh, my feathers are ruined!" she croaked. Then her face lost all its color as she made another discovery. "My voice is ruined, too!" She began to sob pitifully, wondering what her life would be like now.

The parrot stepped forward and spoke for them all. "You are a genuine hero, cuckoo, and you showed great courage. Such selfless behavior surely deserves a suitable reward," he said. "You should rest for a while. We will talk among ourselves and determine how best to repay you."

While the cuckoo nestled into the cave for a nap, the other birds crowded together at the shoreline to determine the best reward for the cuckoo. Every bird had something to say. They whispered, burbled, and squawked. They talked about the large pile of seed that the cuckoo had gathered, and they wondered how she had managed to do so much work alone.

"Cuckoo worked very hard," said the parrot, "risking her life so that we all would survive. For once she didn't think of her beauty or her singing voice, and she showed more bravery than any other bird in the forest." The others nodded in agreement. But what could they offer the cuckoo that would equal the value of the live-giving seeds?

Finally, the birds arrived at a decision. They reasoned that the little cuckoo had worked so hard for them that she should never have to work as hard again. The parrot went to get the cuckoo so that the group could tell her their decision.

Soon the drab cuckoo stood again before the other forest birds. Soot still covered her feathers. "All the birds here owe you a great debt, cuckoo," began the toucan, "and this is how we'd like to repay you. From this day on, you can lay your eggs in any bird's nest. That bird will raise your young as its own."

Cuckoo smiled. Slowly she nodded her head, gracefully accepting the gift.

This is why, even today, the cuckoo is not as brightly colored as the other birds of the Yucatán and does not sing as beautifully as they. It is also why she lays her eggs in other birds' nests.